THE MYSTERY OF THE Lost Colony

First Edition ©2010 Carole Marsh/Gallopade International/Peachtree City, GA
Current Edition ©November 2014
Ebook Edition ©2011
All rights reserved.
Manufactured in Peachtree City, GA

Carole Marsh Mysteries™ and its skull colophon are the property of Carole Marsh and
Gallopade International.

Published by Gallopade International/Carole Marsh Books. Printed in the United States
of America.

Editor: Janice Baker
Cover Design: Vicki DeJoy
Cover Photo Credit: Roanoke Island Festival Park
Content Design: Randolyn Friedlander

Gallopade International is introducing SAT words that kids need to know in
each new book that we publish. The SAT words are bold in the story. Look
for this special logo beside each word in the glossary. Happy Learning!

Gallopade is proud to be a member and supporter of these educational organizations
and associations:

American Booksellers Association
American Library Association
International Reading Association
National Association for Gifted Children
The National School Supply and Equipment Association
The National Council for the Social Studies
Museum Store Association
Association of Partners for Public Lands
Association of Booksellers for Children
Association for the Study of African American Life and History
National Alliance of Black School Educators

Christina *Mimi* *Papa* *Grant*

Once upon a time...

Hmm, kids keep asking me to write a mystery book. What shall I do?

Mimi

Write one about spiders!

On the *Mystery Girl* airplane ...

I can FLY us anywHere!

Or aboard
the *Mimi!*

Take me to the
Forbidden City!

Or by surfboard,
rickshaw,
motorbike,
camel ...

All great ideas!
I can put a lot of history,

MYSTERY,

legend, lore, and laughs in
the books! We can use other boys and girls
in the books. It will be educational and fun!

Good
stuff!

And so, Mimi, Papa, Christina, and Grant took off aboard the *Mystery Girl* and America's National Mystery Book Series—where the adventure is real and so are the characters! —was born.

START YOUR ADVENTURE TODAY!

READ THE BOOK!

GO ONLINE!

TRACK YOUR ADVENTURES!

APPLY TO BE A CHARACTER!

Yikes! That was close!

Rats!

Table of Contents

POOR LITTLE MYSTERY GIRL

MIMI sat on her surfboard-red suitcase and sighed. "Well, this has never happened before," she said, shaking her blond hair. She sighed again.

Papa had just come out of the Falcon Field airplane hangar to give them the bad news: "The Mystery Girl is done broke down and ain't fixable anytime soon."

Mimi wagged her finger at him. "That's awful English!"

"I know," Papa said. "I'm just repeating **verbatim** what the mechanic told me."

Papa, Mimi's husband, the cowboy pilot, waved his cowboy hat over his sweating face. His *usual neatly-pressed jeans were wrinkled, the knees black with grease. His cowboy boots were scuffed.*

"Are you sure they can't do something?" Christina asked. She felt like she could cry. They had been planning this trip to the Outer Banks of North Carolina for a long time. She and her brother Grant often went on mystery research and writing trips with their grandparents, but this one was special.

"Maybe I could take a look?" Grant said, crawling out of a lounge seat where he had fallen asleep during the couple of hours they had been waiting to see the fate of Papa's little red and white airplane.

"Right, Grant!" Christina said with a snort. She was tired, too, and irritable.

"C'mon, hoss," Papa said and scribbled his knuckles through Grant's unruly hair. "Let's both go take a look."

As the "men" stalked off, Christina hopped up from her perch overlooking the tarmac and slung her arm around her grandmother's shoulder. "I'm sorry, Mimi," she said. "I know this was going to be a special trip."

Mimi sighed and yawned. "Yes, I was sure looking forward to showing you and Grant all the wonderful places Papa and I enjoyed when we lived up in eastern North Carolina."

"And where you started writing mystery books, right?" Christina asked.

Mimi sighed AGAIN. "Yes. That was more than thirty years ago. Back when your mother and your Uncle Michael were the real kid characters in my mysteries. We met so many nice people, and I often used some of their children in some of my books, after your mom and Uncle Michael got too old to be in them."

"And before Grant and I came along, right?" Christina said with a smile.

"Yes, thank goodness for grandchildren!" Mimi said and laughed. "And now, even your cousins Avery, Ella, and Evan are getting old enough to be in the mysteries."

"Hey, you aren't going to boot Grant and me out of the books are you?" Christina asked, **feigning** *horror at the idea.*

Mimi frowned and stood up. "Stand up!" she ordered. Christina did and they stood side by side, looking at their reflection in the large panes of glass overlooking the runways. "You are taller than I am!"

Now it was Christina's turn to sigh. She was a lot taller than her grandmother! But she had been in the Carole Marsh Mystery books for a lot of years. Would that come to an end one day soon? She guessed all things must change.

Before she could ponder her thoughts to some undesired conclusion, Papa and Grant trudged back into the terminal.

"The Mystery Girl is done broke down and ain't fixable anytime soon," Grant said with a thick, country accent.

"Grant!" Mimi said. "Speak proper English!"

Grant shook his head. "I'm just repeating what the mechanic said. Papa is right; we aren't going anywhere, anyway, anyhow, any time."

Papa nodded at Mimi's raised hopeful eyebrows. It was almost dark and they all were starving. Originally, they'd planned to leave mid-morning and get to Manteo, check into the inn, go for a swim, and be sitting down at some wonderful restaurant with fried shrimp and hushpuppies about now.

Suddenly and simultaneously, everyone's stomach growled loudly.

Mimi dusted off her red skirt and jacket. "Well, I tell you what. Let's write ourselves a better ending than this. I'm sure Papa has the mechanic working hard on the plane, so why don't we grab some pizza and take it home. While we are waiting for parts, repairs, and some good weather luck"—it had started to rain—"we can camp out by our big fireplace, and I'll tell you all about The Mystery of the Lost Colony."

"Great idea!" said Christina. She'd had enough of the airport and its one vending machine.

"If food is involved, I'll follow!" Grant agreed, rubbing his stomach as if winding up a propeller.

"I'm a' gettin' the car!" Papa said and dashed out into the rain.

As Mimi and the kids donned their jackets and huddled by the exit waiting for the car to appear, they did not see a grubby mechanic peer out from the hangar and give them a "good riddance" smirk.

PIZZA AND A MOVIE

"Back at the ranch," as Papa called his and Mimi's large, rambling home in the center of Peachtree City, they dashed in the house with two large pizzas, trying to "run between the raindrops," like Papa suggested.

"Meatosaurus for us men!" Grant said, slamming one of the pizza boxes on the kitchen table. "Vegeterrible for you girls."

"I'm so hungry I could eat my cowboy hat," Papa swore. Instead, they each shed their coats, washed their hands, and grabbed one of the paper plates Mimi dished out faster than flying Frisbees.

Since the power had gone out, Papa got a big fire going, Mimi lit some candles, and they indeed did "camp out" to chow down as Mimi began her story from the past:

"I always did want to be a mystery book writer," Mimi said, and her grandchildren could see in her eyes a movie from the past unfolding in her mind. "I wanted to write mysteries for kids. I loved reading mysteries when I was a little girl— Nancy Drew and Hardy Boys. When your mom was Christina's age and Uncle Michael was Grant's age, I decided to give it a try."

"The Mystery of Blackbeard the Pirate, right?" Christina asked. Mimi nodded.

"I didn't stop to consider what if I was successful," Mimi said with a laugh. "So when kids loved the book and begged for more, well, I had to really hurry up and turn into a full-time mystery writer, and one with a great, handsome, helpful assistant!"

They all stared at Papa, who beamed, even as he continued to chew on a big piece of pepperoni pizza. Mimi blew him a kiss and Grant made a gagging sound.

"Ignore the Great Grant, Mimi," Christina said. "Tell us more."

Mimi wiped her mouth daintily. "Well, as I wrote a few more mysteries, it got to be time for a very historic event in early American history—the 400th anniversary of the Lost Colony. And everyone suggested I set a mystery in Manteo and on the Outer Banks so kids could learn about what happened. And so I did."

Grant's eyes were wide. Pizza sauce was smeared from his chin to his eyebrow, but he didn't seem to notice. "A LOST colony? Why was it lost? How did it get lost? Did it ever get found? And what is a colony? And where was it? Who lived there? And..."

"Whoa, little buddy!" Papa said. "Let me go make some of my famous cowboy cocoa and Mimi will tell you all about it." He rose to go to the kitchen.

Grant was still wide-eyed.   "Papa?" he whispered.

"Yes?" his grandfather answered, stretching to get the kinks of out his back.

"Would you hurry...please!"

THE LOST COLONY

As the hour of midnight drew near and the fire settled to a deep red glow, they all drew closer and covered up with afghans as they sipped their hot chocolate, dotted with marshmallows, and listened to Mimi's tale:

"You have to imagine the coastland of America four hundred years ago," she said. "Of course, it wasn't America yet. It was known as the New World. At least that's what explorers called it. The British and the Spanish and other nations sailed big ships through the high seas trying to be the first to discover and claim new lands for their countries.

"Picture what would become America just sitting here—an abundance of waters, coastlands, mountains, wildlife, and other natural resources—riches, indeed, to any nation wanting to expand its borders. Great Britain, for example, was chomping at the bit to get over here and check it out! A couple of early reconnaissance parties were sent over and word came back that the New World was a wonderland!"

Papa interrupted. "Well, they forgot to mention mosquitoes the size of dinner plates, untamed forestland, the heat and humidity, and, of course, the savages."

Now, Grant's eyes were really wide. "Savages?" he whispered to himself.

"Those whose names were terrible!" Mimi added, earnestly nodding her head. "I know it's hard to believe, but believe me." Now, even Christina was curious and Mimi went on:

"Then Queen Elizabeth and Sir Walter Raleigh got serious. They decided to send a real ship over, and not just with explorers, but with enough people—men, women, and children—to try to set up a permanent colony and see if they could survive here in the New World.

"The party set sail aboard the good ship Elizabeth. It was a long journey across the Atlantic Ocean. Nautical instruments were rare and elementary and so navigation was still done by the stars, though the captain of this ship used a cross-staff.

"Just imagine them finally arriving, all decked out in their heavy English clothes and boots, trying to navigate through the puzzlelike maze of sandy shoals and banks that changed with each tide. They were tired, hungry, and some ill—one young woman very, very pregnant. They finally came ashore in what today we call North Carolina. The shore was thick with snarled forests. They had to hatchet their way inland and figure out where to set up camp. This was near the town that would one day be called Manteo."

"And that was the Lost Colony?" Grant asked, unable to wait any longer.

Mimi put her finger to her lips with a shhhhhh. "Not yet," she added and continued.

"They did establish a colony. But they were not alone. There were Native Americans already living here. It was uncertain how they would feel about usurpers upon their land. But the colonists had a lot of things to worry about."

"Like what?!" Christina asked, already figuring out that the so-called "savages" and "those whose names were terrible" were the Indians, at least that's what the English people would have called them.

"Like starving to death!" Mimi said. "They finally had to send the ship back for supplies. It would take a long time for the ship to return to England and then get back to America. The colonists were not sure that they could survive that long.

"John White was especially worried about leaving his daughter Eleanor behind. She was the young woman who'd been pregnant and had given birth to the first English child born in the New World—Virginia Dare."

"What happened, Mimi? What happened?!" both kids squealed at once. Papa just smiled and waited.

"Well," Mimi began, looking sad. "The supplies were fetched and the ship returned, but the colonists were all gone. All that was found was a single sign that read 'CROATOAN.' No one knew if that meant a place they might have gone, or some native peoples who might have taken them in, or, if..." Mimi stopped. The fire groaned.

"If what, Mimi?" Christina pleaded, fearing the answer.

"Or, if they had all been killed—men, women, children, and even baby Virginia," Mimi finished. She said no more.

Grant sat straight up. He was not used to this kind of story. And, he was very tenderhearted. He flung his arms about wildly, as if acting out a scene. "But they found them, right? They sent out a search party and looked, and they found them, and they were all right, right, right, Mimi?"

Mimi shook her head slowly. "No, Grant, they never did find them. And that is why 'til this day they are known as the Lost Colony. And that's why I thought it would make a great setting for a mystery story!"

Papa startled them all by clapping his hands loudly. "Okay, buckaroos! Bedtime! It's past midnight, and for all we know, the Mystery Girl might be fixed by morning, so round 'em up and head 'em out to bed." He pointed to the loft room where the kids slept when they overnighted.

"But..." Christina began, even as she arose. Papa always said what he meant and meant what he said.

"BUT..." Grant started, and then yawned.

"No ifs, ands, or buts!" Papa insisted. And soon, all were in bed asleep, the fire fizzled out, and the rain continued. Over at the airport, the Mystery Girl sat in darkness in the hangar, no one working on her at all.

UNSETTLED DREAMS

That night, Christina slept fitfully. She had studied a lot of American history so far in school, but she did not recall the story of the Lost Colony. It seemed so sad. In her dreams, she imagined Eleanor Dare getting along with the Native American women. They sat on straw mats in the shade, rocking their babies, like Virginia, and learning each other's language, even giggling when they made mistakes.

Grants dreams were vivid. In his mind, mayhem swept the coastland as the colonists and

Indians made sneak attacks on each other. The colonists tried to poison the natives and the natives fought with weapons made from sharp oyster shells tied to sticks. There was blood, and Grant even woke up once, moaning and sweating. But he was so exhausted, he soon fell back to sleep, dreaming in a language he could not understand.

The next morning, the kids awoke to the sounds and scents of a roaring fire and bacon sizzling in Papa's cowboy frying pan. Soon they were all gathered around the kitchen table eating by candlelight. The power was still out.

"I'm heading over to Falcon Field to check on the Mystery Girl," Papa said, swiping his plate clean and refilling his coffee cup to the brim. He kissed Mimi on the top of her head, waved at the kids, slapped on his cowboy hat, and headed out into the nasty weather, whistling.

"Mimi?" Christina said. "Since we're stuck indoors this nasty morning, please tell us what you wrote about the Lost Colony!" Both cheeks bulging with food like a hoarding squirrel, Grant nodded. Mimi did too. She sipped her hot tea and said:

"Because of another book I wrote, I met the man who would become the head of a historic site in Manteo. He invited Papa and me to come there and see the building of the Elizabeth II, a replica of the ship that had brought the colonists to North Carolina."

"Was that for the 400th anniversary?" Christina guessed, and Mimi nodded.

"We had a great trip to Manteo and Nags Head and all around the Outer Banks. We met a lot of nice folks, some of whom were descended from the early English settlers—not the Lost Colonists, but later settlers. Some of these people still spoke in a strong Elizabethan accent. I had to listen closely to know what they were saying."

"What kind of words did they use?" Christina asked.

Mimi thrummed her fingers on the table as she recalled, "Oh, words like hoigh for high and toide for tide."

Grant giggled. "Sounds silly to me," he said, toast crumbs spewing from his lips.

"Reeeaaaallly, Grant!" his sister complained. "No one knows, or does, silly like you do!"

Mimi ignored them. "That's the way the English talked. These Manteo locals told me a lot of legends, like about the wild ponies of the Outer Banks, and..."

Grant interrupted. "But did they tell you whichaway the Lost Colonists went?"

"No, Grant," Mimi insisted. "That's why it's a real-life mystery." Grant frowned. He had never thought about there being real-life mysteries. He just knew the kind Mimi made up for her books. The thought bothered him.

"The book?" Christina reminded.

"Oh, yes," Mimi said. "I picked a couple of local kids to be characters and began to write. This gave Papa and me a great excuse to stay in Manteo for awhile in an old Elizabethan, Tudor-style inn, and to participate in some of the quadricentennial activities."

"THA' WHAT?" Grant asked.

"That means four hundred years," Christina said smugly.

Grant stared at her in amazement. "How did you know that silver-dollar word?"

Christina shrugged. "I guessed. But I got it right!" She turned back to her grandmother who was now cleaning off the table. "So what was the story about, Mimi?"

Mimi stared out at the rain. "I tell you what," she said. "You kids help me clean up, and to pass the time, we'll adjourn by the fire, and I'll read the book aloud to you."

THE MYSTERY OF THE Lost Colony

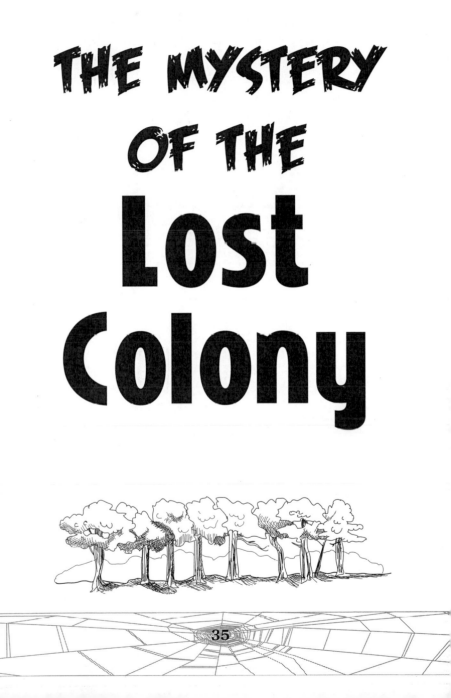

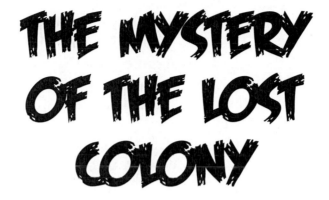

THE MYSTERY OF THE LOST COLONY

Preface

Jeremy and Dennis stood in the stifling bathroom with the door closed and the lights off. There was the sound of ripping paper.

"Your mom's downstairs waiting for you," Jeremy said impatiently.

"I know, I know," Dennis yowled, "but we gotta see if it works."

Giggles. Crunching. The bathroom mirror told the truth.

"Yiiiii!" Dennis squealed.

"It does work!" Jeremy cried, chewing the wintergreen Life Savers as hard and as fast as he could. Faint sparks of light flashed in the mirror.

"It's like an edible video game," Dennis said.

"Must be some kind of physics," Jeremy gurgled between gnashes.

Dennis choked and his friend pounded him on the back. Suddenly the door flew open and the light snapped on. Perplexed, Jeremy's father stared at the boys with their mouths hanging open, eyes wide, sticky saliva dripping from their front teeth like mad dogs. He wriggled his nose at the smell.

Jeremy's mouth slammed shut. With a wink to his friend, Dennis went out. Mr. Mydet sighed, turned out the light, and closed the bathroom door in his son's face.

Jeremy giggled, popped another candy into his mouth and began chewing again. He heard the fading voices . . . the slam of the door . . . the start of the car motor . . . and as the first spark appeared in the mirror—the scream!

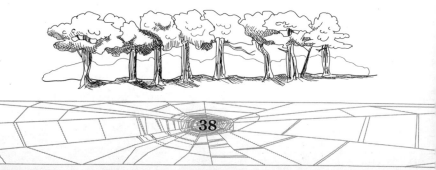

1
MIDNIGHT, ROANOKE ISLAND

Jeremy lay curled like a cold clam beneath Grandma Mary's quilt. Never in his twelve years of perfectly normal life on Roanoke Island had he ever felt such fear and misery.

A loose board banged the tin roof of the old house like a warning. He shivered. Why did he ever beg to have this small cold room off the attic?

He didn't mind ghosts. But real spooks snooping and stealing only a few feet away from him—now, that was scary.

They'd only discovered the disappearance a few hours ago. Someone from the 400th Anniversary Committee had come by to see if Grandma Mary had any old pictures of Manteo. Even over a year ahead, everyone in North Carolina was preparing to celebrate America's first English colony that had vanished—men, women, and children—without a trace.

The groaning attic was filled with crackly, yellowed photographs of everything from the Mighty Midgetts of Chicamacomico who'd saved many a shipwrecked sailor's life to the horse-drawn buggies that used to cart people over the giant sand dunes at Jockey's Ridge to their seaside cottage retreats. Grandma had hoisted her skirts, marched proudly up the attic stairs—then screamed.

The small leather deerskin trunk was empty. She wanted to show them one of Grandpa's 100 commemorative coins struck in 1937—350 years after the birth of Virginia Dare—the first English child born in the New World. When Grandpa had shown the coins to Jeremy and promised they'd be his on his eighteenth birthday, the cache had glistened like pirate booty.

Jeremy looked out at the silver coin moon. As clouds curled over the orb, he pictured the trunk empty of all the silver half-dollars Grandpa Joe had bought in 1937 that were now worth more than $500 each.

He didn't know if he felt worse that an **heirloom** had been snatched from his family or that it had been swiped from a room just the other side of his head—and he never heard a thing.

The loose board banged again. Short blond hairs stood at attention on his arms. Jeremy dug deep into the covers. He had to sleep, for tomorrow was going to be the second most miserable day in his, until now, ordinary, wintergreen Life Saver life.

2
MORNING,
ROANOKE
ISLAND

Jeremy's best friend, Dennis, had come over on the early ferry from Ocracoke Island and was shocked at the news of the theft. With the golden brilliance of the tiger eye rings which washed ashore occasionally, his eyes flew to each adult in search of the make-everything-right answers expected of them, but they were busy choreographing breakfast around the big kitchen table, making sure the dumbstruck visitor got one of everything.

"For 400 years we've had mostly peace and quiet on the Outer Banks," crooned Grandma Mary, sadly.

"You call blood-thirsty pirating, Indian attacks, Civil War battles, and ships crashing on sandbars peace and quiet?" asked Dad.

Grandma Mary retreated behind her coffee cup. Jeremy tried to change the subject. "That dumb speech I have to write is about the Indians," he grumbled.

"You mean savages," his father hissed.

Jeremy groaned. "The white men were the savages. They ran the Indians off their land, brought diseases they had no immunity to, falsely accused them of stealing, and killed their king, Wingina. I'd retaliate too!"

"Does your speech have a title yet?" asked Mother quickly.

"Those-Whose-Names-Were-Terrible," Jeremy intoned dramatically. "I announced it yesterday in class. Frankly, my title is longer than my speech right now."

"We can never make it up to native Americans," Grandma said.

"Why not?" asked Dennis between bites.

"That's a good question," said Jeremy. "I hope that's what my speech will be about, if I finish."

Jeremy's father gave him an amused look. "Oh, I think Ms. Phillips will see that you're ready to give it by the 400th celebration."

"Speaking of savages," Dennis muttered under his breath.

"The coins vanished," Grandma said wearily. "Just like the Lost Colony."

"I sure hope not," Jeremy said. "They never found it."

Silently, everyone went on eating. Grandpa Joe's empty chair creaked as audibly as if someone had just settled into it.

"Let's go, Den," Jeremy said suddenly and reached for his jacket.

3
MORNING, MANTEO

Jeremy and Dennis stared up at the big-bellied hull of the Elizabeth II. The 400th Committee was building a replica of the ship the colonists sailed to the New World. Jeremy's daily rounds included The Christmas Shop, Good Luck Street, and The House by the Side of the Road, but he always wound up on Manteo's waterfront so he could survey the noisy progress in the boathouse.

Astride their rickety, salt-air-rusted bikes, the boys eased up to the ragged sand fence encircling the construction area. Jeremy inhaled deeply. The smell of the fresh cut juniper and pine was warm and sweet. Hunched shipwrights labored as the clang of the blacksmith jarred their tasks. Jeremy scooped up a handful of wood shavings and stuffed them into his pocket.

"Why did you do that?" Dennis asked.

"For a memento or souvenir—a real one, not like a bumper sticker or tee shirt," Jeremy said.

"That's a great idea," said Dennis, grabbing a handful of the soft blond curls for himself. "I bet I can sell them for a buck apiece."

Jeremy started to complain that non-commercialism was what he meant, but just then, the captain stormed out of the boathouse. "Well, I just don't know . . ." he said to the young carpenter trailing him. "I sure didn't order the hold sealed yet. No one has permission to touch this ship without my ok." He looked like he'd rip the belly of the ship back open in a heartbeat.

The carpenter slapped his hands helplessly against his tool apron. "I guess they did it yesterday when we all were in Raleigh." He shrugged his shoulders and walked off.

Ignoring the boys, the two adults stalked along the shore of Shallowbag Bay, eyeing the Elizabeth II as though it were a caged animal about to break loose.

"Wonder what that's all about?" asked Dennis from his perch in a puddle of sawdust.

"No telling," said Jeremy. He walked toward the water, one foot in front of the other as if towed by an invisible rope. It was only because he was a collector—stamps, bottles, wood shavings—anything—that he even noticed it. The pale March sun spewing between the rib slats of fence winked against something embedded in the sand. He reached down and, sawdust trickling through his fingers, gingerly retrieved the glistening object—a 1937 Virginia Dare coin.

4
NEW YEAR'S, KILL DEVIL HILLS

Summer skidded by. Fall fell. The cold claws of winter gripped the coast. The monstrous sand dune was as cold and gray as a beached whale. Jeremy and Dennis watched the candy-apple sun plop into the sound and the cotton candy sky fade to the deep purple of nightfall.

Jeremy didn't know who spied it first, but suddenly they were grinning and running across the top of the dune to the deserted hang glider. Cautiously, they explored the abandoned moth.

"We could fly it," Dennis whispered.

"We could crash, too," Jeremy said, but Dennis was already rigging himself into the central cocoon.

Now the left wing butted the ground, now the right wing pointed skyward. Each movement forced Jeremy backwards. A sudden updraft lurched the winged boy forward and out into the thin air. He squealed in surprise and delight.

"Come back here," Jeremy ordered, sounding strangely like his father.

"I can't," the faint cry echoed as the distance between them grew. A gust sucked the small boy up into the deadly dusk. Like the Cheshire cat, his grin seemed the last gleam to leave each space he occupied momentarily before advancing upward.

Jeremy pursued the sand-bound shadow. For a moment, the boys were caught in the same exhilarating sky/dune dance that Orville and Wilbur Wright had experienced another cold winter's day on these dunes long ago.

Then, the reality of gravity and danger gripped Jeremy's aching legs back to Earth. As the great gaping mouth of darkness swallowed the dune, he crashed knees and chest upon the sand. The beautiful butterfly became a bat, black wings battering the night sky, swooping lower and lower between the dunes, a bloodsucker seeking its supper.

"Dennis," Jeremy called, "Come down. Come down, now!" If only you were a kite, he thought, I could reel you in. But bats have a mind of their own.

The wind was beating now, the dunes a surf set in steadily breaking waves. A cloud of sand swatted him in the face. And when he rubbed the grit from his eyes, the glider was gone!

5
THE NIGHTBAT

Neither star nor moon marred the black puddle overhead. Heels first, Jeremy skidded frantically down the dune. He stared across the sea of sand into the void of water. But the behemoth dinosaur backs lay sleeping, and if the Roanoke Sound had swallowed its prey, there were no concentric circles of confession.

Then among the bumpy beasts . . . amidst the stiff hairs of sea oats fringing their backs, sprawled the fallen bat, barely fluttering in the night wind.

As fast as you can with every dead sailor and pirate grabbing at your soles from their sandy graves, Jeremy ran. To rescue a boy, who did not move, trapped in a tangled web of leather, face down in the suffocating sand.

Jeremy's progress across the endless crests and valleys was slow. He felt he was riding an elevator to cross the street. As he trudged on through the surf of sand he spied a flicker of light, a glimmer turned glow by the time he mounted the next wave. By its direction and speed, it was tracking the same prey.

This night mare was a legendary steed. All banker boys grew up knowing the legend of how the riff-raff of long ago would tie a lantern to the neck of a Banks pony and lead it across the sand-ridge to trick the sailors at sea. Spying the bobbing light, they would steer forth toward safety only to founder on the shifting shoals of the Graveyard of the Atlantic and be dashed upon the sand, then plundered by the laughing leader of the Nag's Head.

It's only a legend, Jeremy reminded himself. Like a mirage, I only think I see it. But the next dark breath of wind brought an evil neigh to the doorstep of his sunken feet.

By the time he reached the water's edge, there was only empty sand. No bat. No nag.

No Dennis. Only a faint whinny that could have been beast or boy. Jeremy laid his head on the enormous pillow of sand and cried.

6
HOME

The sun sprawled through the window upon the numb body hung across the bed. Jeremy did not remember getting home. He awakened from his nightmare to see his arms aglow with glittering fish scales. Two pale puddles of diamonds dripped from his shoes. He peeked into his mirror and discovered he was now blond.

When he stood up, there was an audible sprinkle of sand from his body onto the floor. "Have to find a way to get the vacuum up here," he thought, then grimaced. "Worried about sand and vacuums, you idiot, when your best friend is missing?"

He dashed into the bathroom, grabbed a towel, yanked open the shower door, lunged inside–and screamed. A body was propped in the corner of the shower. At first, Jeremy feared he was dead. But his cry brought movement from the mound of muddy boy.

Gently, Jeremy touched his friend. Dennis groaned. A watery blue eye, bloodshot as a treasure map, opened, then clinked shut. "C'mon, boy," Jeremy pleaded, trying to lift him from the tub. Even a kid as scrawny as Dennis weighed a small ton as a lifeless lump. The other flimsy eyelid hoisted itself to half-mast and a bloody crowfoot eyeball rolled back and forth in its sandy socket.

"Cut it out!" Jeremy insisted in a stern whisper. He was near panic. What was wrong with Dennis? He didn't act like he was asleep; he acted like he'd been drugged.

"That's it," Jeremy thought. "Dennis didn't get here by himself. He was drugged!"

"Drubbed and drubbed," Dennis muttered, then giggled uncontrollably, in spite of a painful frown.

"Sssh," Jeremy pleaded. With the tip of his finger he propped one eyelid open, then the other. "Try to stay awake. You're right—you were drugged, then dragged here."

Disconcerted, Jeremy looked at the opening to the attic. Twice now, at least, someone, somehow had sneaked into his home, invaded his rooms and done bad things. But how and why? Why his money and his friend? Something strange was going on, but he could prove nothing.

"I don't know . . . I don't know what happened," Dennis repeated to Jeremy's persistent question.

It was the only answer there seemed to be at this time.

7
AN ICY
OUTER BANKS

The beach is different in winter. Things are always stark on the banks, but in winter, the gray of the sky and sand and water run together in an extra-depressing bleakness.

As they streaked down the wilted gray velvet ribbon of highway, Jeremy had a clammy feeling. His brain felt like a tangled nest of eels and his heart was cold as an oyster.

The Hatteras Lighthouse was shrouded in fog and the ferry looked more like a funeral barge than a ferry. Across the water, Ocracoke, the outermost island of the Outer Banks, always remote, forlorn, seemed even more so today.

Mist licked the back of his neck like a cat's cold tongue, and Jeremy tugged his windbreaker tighter. He watched the twin, demon eyes of the tail lights of his mother's car vanish in the white swirl. Thank goodness she'd just thought Dennis was sleepy.

They boarded the groaning ferry. Grouchy gulls sneered at empty-handed passengers. The few passengers huddled in the passenger lounge and stared out into the torrent of clouds.

A horse trailer held two of the famous Ocracoke wild ponies, huddled together against the wringing wind. Jeremy nudged his zombie friend. "C'mon, let's look at the ponies." Maybe some fresh air would help him recover from the effects of the drug before his mother saw him and got suspicious.

On deck, Dennis reached out and patted the sea biscuit marking on the forehead of one whining pony. Then it happened. The gate was open! Thrilled with their freedom, the ponies charged wildly around the slippery deck. If they jumped the railing like it was their pen . . .

Their keeper charged out of the wheelhouse in a rage. Jeremy caught one pony, but Dennis just stood in the same spot, not even budging when the sea biscuit pony's hoof reared dangerously close to his head.

When the animals were finally captured, Jeremy endured the keeper's tirade of accusations. "You boys are in big trouble," he ranted. Dennis's strange behavior didn't help anything, and only the insistence of a passenger that the boys hadn't touched the latch got them off the hook—for now. But for how long, Jeremy wondered?

It appeared Ocracoke would be no haven. Their problems—whoever they were—were as close as their shadows.

8
OCRACOKE

They were greeted on the far shore by another lonesome stretch of highway smothered in shallow puddles of seawater washed over the dunes at the last high tide. The ferry master gave them a ride to the village and dropped them off at one of the shut-eyed cottages.

Inside, Jeremy's spirits lifted. The house was aglow with a roaring fire, and the smell of warm cinnamon. Red ribbon-bedecked yaupon festooned every corner. Tiny white lights winked merrily on the tree.

With a crumb-wreathed smile, Dennis's little sister Julie handed him a cookie. "Hot,

Jerm," she warned with a shy giggle and scampered off.

Jeremy and Dennis shed their fog-coated coats and flopped on the floor in front of the fire. Spewing sugar snowflakes, Dennis, now wide-awake, begged: "What's going on? What do you think happened? Why . . . how? How come?"

"Dunno, Den," Jeremy said. "We were just tricked, but how and why, I can't figure out. What have I done to get someone on my case like this?"

"Have you made someone at school mad?" asked Dennis.

"Always!" said Jeremy. "Especially Ms. Phillips since I haven't finished my speech for the Four Hundredth Anniversary celebration."

"Why not?" asked Dennis.

Jeremy groaned. "You try and write a speech to give in front of thousands of people that insults them and their ancestors about how bad they treated—and still treat—the Indians! Ms. Phillips wants me to tell the truth, but she doesn't want me to make anybody angry. I don't think it's possible on this subject."

"Maybe you've made some Indian mad," Dennis speculated.

"I don't know any Indians," Jeremy said. "At least not that I know of. But if they've had anything to do with grandpa's missing coins and kidnapping and drugging you, then they are savages!"

Dennis rolled over onto his stomach and looked up at his friend in dismay. "Well, if those savages were the ones who let the ponies loose on the ferry, then . . ." he began.

Jeremy completed the dreadful thought, ". . . then they're on the island too!"

BACK IN MIMI'S KITCHEN...

"Wow!" Grant gasped. "Is Jeremy ok?"

Christina said, "Grant, Mimi always says you have to hear the rest of the story. You know she won't tell us! That's how she keeps kids reading her books...she makes us, even if we have to get out the flashlight and read under the covers and get in trouble with Mom and Dad."

Mimi laughed. "That's right! My job is to keep you reading, but it also keeps me writing—I want to know what happens."

"So there really is a Manteo, North Carolina?" Grant asked.

Soon, they were back in the kitchen and Mimi poured another cup of coffee and sat down at the table. Her grandchildren used that as their cue to sit down and listen.

"Yes, silly," said Christina. "That's where we were going to fly into, if the Mystery Girl hadn't broken down."

"Settle down," Mimi said, "and I'll tell you more. Papa and I have been to Manteo a lot. It is a small fishing village and a tourist town that is a gateway to the Outer Banks. Because they have so much English Tudor architecture, it looks like a little town near London during Shakespeare's day."

"Who's Sheik's spear?" asked Grant.

"That's another story for another day, Grant," Christina said. "Keep going, Mimi, please."

Mimi sipped her coffee and nodded. "Papa and I went to the grand opening of the lovely new historic site in Manteo one year, which gave me an idea for this story. We always loved to visit Manteo, especially to see the Lost Colony outdoor drama and the Elizabethan Gardens. Today, the Elizabeth II is docked at Shallowbag Bay on Ice Plant Island. It just seemed like everywhere I turned was good mystery book fodder."

"But is Jeremy in big trouble, or not?" Grant demanded to know.

Mimi felt sorry for her sweet, tenderhearted grandson. "Let's keep reading, Grant, and find out."

9
TEACH'S HOLE

Revitalized by fire and food, the fur of their coats dry, the boys set out to explore.

Everything was still the same. That was part of the charm and security of the windblown island. The bankers, ever at the mercy of Mother Nature's whims, made a point to keep the old buildings, the old ways, intact. Many still spoke the Elizabethan English of their ancestors.

Whooping with joy, they scooted around the sandy paths, through the tight knots of yaupon. The ferry had returned from its sojourn to Swan Quarter and flopped in exhausted anchor near the Coast Guard Station.

Lights twinkled in the dusk, evidence that the utility company was still doing its best. Regularly, the power to the island vanished as though the electricity brought on the lines and poles which stitched the Outer Banks together had run aground in the sand. No one missed a beat as candles were handily found and sparked. Usually, there were more groans than cheers from the tourists when the stray current finally found its way back.

With fog-muffled giggles, the boys raced around Silver Lake to the toy-size lighthouse. Here, at Teach's Hole, the pirate Blackbeard had lost his head in his final, bloody battle, and the boys always checked to see if it had washed ashore.

The fog pushed them around the familiar intertwined lanes. Beneath the low umbrellas of the thick green hammocks, night was settling to lay in wait for them.

They hastened caddy-corner from one snatch of cord grass to another, trying to outfox the fog in pursuit of the next landmark.

"Here we are," Dennis said. Even the skinny slits of sand fence surrounding the graveyard were tufted with wads of fog that also swirled in white halos around the tombstones of the British soldiers who'd found their final home here.

Dennis was the first to see the **atrocity**. The marble markers were swiped with wide swatches of red.

Gingerly, Jeremy touched one cockeyed stone with the tips of his fingers. "It's wet," he said. "Somebody just did it."

Dennis pulled his hand beneath the streetlight. "It's blood!"

Behind them roared an evil laugh. And before they could turn, the power went out.

10
AWFUL
OCRACOKE

"I'm sick of it, Den!" Jeremy said, as they huddled in bed trying to keep warm 'til the power came back on—whenever that would be.

"Of what?" Dennis asked.　His eyes darted to the window, the flickering eye of the candle's reflection stared back at him.

Jeremy kicked the quilt in aggravation. "I want to know who's trying to scare us and why."

He, too, wondered if they were out there in the dark—watching and laughing.　The boys had jumped the fence and ran toward the Island Inn, certain they heard footsteps behind them, but too afraid to turn and peer into the blinding darkness.

Just then, after a few hopeful glimmers, the power returned the night to normal. The boys went downstairs to a sober dinner of tepid clam chowder and rock-hard hushpuppies.

The grandfather clock, not dependent on Vepco Power, had patiently ticked the dark time forward. Jeremy glanced at it as he walked by. "Well," he said to Dennis, "at least we'll know when to leave tomorrow for Old Christmas."

The celebration of Epiphany or Old Christmas on January 6 had origins in the wild, weird, wondrous traditions of the Middle Ages. Legends of the dragon of St. George, the beast of Trent Woods descended from a "Hobby Horse," animals kneeling to pray, poke salad bushes and hopvines sprouting leaves in winter, streams flowing backwards, and woodland creatures dancing in the moonlight, were all part of this event still celebrated in the tiny town of Rodanthe each year.

It might seem backwards and strange to folks in more sophisticated places, but who in their right mind would be foolish enough to argue with hanging up their stockings twice each year, Jeremy wondered as he gulped down his lukewarm glass of milk.

"What's this?" Dennis's dad asked, grabbing Jeremy's hand.

He rubbed the boy's fingers roughly. "Been painting?"

"Uh, no . . ." Jeremy began. "I mean yes," he said.

"He means no, Dad," Dennis assured his father.

The perplexed parents exchanged confused and dubious glances at their son and his friend.

"Old Christmas does strange things to boys," Dennis's mom dismissed the incident with a suspicious smile.

11
OLD
CHRISTMAS

The trip across the Sound on the crowded ferry was invigorating. It was as if they were all hurrying to the past as fast as they could to make sure it was still there, safe and the same—like the present and future could never be. Throngs of families filled the great room of the Rodanthe Hall. Everyone had hibernated in dark homes the night before, and now their excitement and enthusiasm for life with light escaped in hearty laughter and cheerful greetings.

Outside in the cold, velvet sky, winking with winter stars, smoky brush and driftwood bonfires flared gaily and roasting oysters sizzled and steamed. But there were too many old friends to see, too many girls to tease, too many tricks to play, and too much taffy to pull, to stand still long enough to fight an obnoxious oyster shell for its juicy treasure.

Lungs filled with cold night air and leftover laughter, the children were herded inside for the celebration's highlight—the escapades of Old Buck. Against a symphony of coughing, sneezing, and throat-clearing, Mr. Herbert's patient explanation of the tradition was piercingly interrupted by a child's shriek at the glimpse of horns pricking through the black curtain stage right.

Jeremy had the same feeling as when he was little and still peered up the dark chimney in the family room, certain he'd heard the jingling of bells and the stomp of hooves. But Old Buck was better because he was real—even when you knew it was just Bobby Midgett on one end and Sam Herbert at the other.

Though that same small child joy was bottled up inside him, he was too embarrassed to let it out in squeals of delight, but he stood on tiptoe to see Old Buck's entrance. As the lopsided animal cavorted across the stage, Jeremy and Dennis exchanged glances and giggled, relieved to see the other thought it was okay not to get too big to get a kick out of something so hokey.

"Caper, Buck caper!" cried the crowd.

The little children howled and hid behind their mother's legs as the beast descended the steps and paraded through the agitated throng. As he safely passed each child, they bravely patted his spotted backside with a squeal of delight. But Buck ignored them and lowering his horns, moved faster and faster toward Jeremy's midsection. Once more, the lights went out.

12
OLD BUCK

Dennis's shrieked warning came too late. With a painful thud Jeremy felt the head of the beast shove his bellybutton to his backbone, each horn locked against his sides. He gasped in pain and the invisible crowd gave quarter as Buck shoved his captive backwards through the open doors and toward the biggest of the bonfires.

Holding tight to keep his balance, Jeremy could not escape. His surprise and confusion turned to panic as he felt the heat behind him and then himself falling helplessly into it.

But just a few feet from the inferno, a stick of driftwood caught his ankle and he tumbled sideways onto the beach. The front of Old Buck tried desperately to stop, but the blind back half kept pushing and the beast careened into the edge of the fire then scrambled out. The mottled tarp was on fire. Jeremy rolled over in time to see the fabric flutter in flames to the ground and two figures race down the dark beach into the night.

The sudden darkness from the power failure had hidden Old Buck's true intentions and so no one else had realized what happened and just called, "Bye, Buck . . . see you next year."

Only Dennis dashed to Jeremy's aid. "No holes gushin' blood," he reported in relief. "Was it an accident?"

"No accident," moaned Jeremy. "What I don't understand is why whoever was under that tarp tonight called me a savage."

"You're no savage," Dennis assured his friend.

"Gee, thanks, Den, but why does the tail end of a fake bull think I am—that's the question."

OUT BY MIMI'S POOL...

The sun finally popped out and Mimi, Christina, and Grant adjourned from the kitchen table to the patio by the swimming pool.

"It's not fair!" Christina said. "I want to be in this book! The kids are having too much fun."

"Fun?" groused Grant. "It's too scary for me. I'm glad we're here, high and dry."

"You won't be if I push you in the pool," teased Christina.

"Just try, big sister, just try," Grant warned, putting up his fists.

Mimi ignored them. She spoke almost as if daydreaming. "Yes, Christina, I do wish you could have seen Kill Devil Hill by moonlight. It's so eerie beneath a full moon. You just feel history seeping up out of the sand with the day's heat. You can see the ocean waves crashing in the distance and are reminded of all the shipwrecks off the coast."

Grant looked puzzled. "So you didn't make up everything in the book?"

Mimi laughed. "Of course not, Grant. You know that. If you read a fact, it's true. Sometimes the truth is just stranger than fiction!"

"Remember when we read The Mystery at Kill Devil Hills, Grant?" Christina said.

"Yeah," Grant answered. "We learned all about Orville and Wilbur Wright and the first flight. But I'm a member of the 'Man Will Never Fly Society,'" he teased.

"Sure, Grant," said his sister. "So that's why you're always first aboard the Mystery Girl?"

"And the last off!" Grant agreed. "Hey, Mimi, I'm hungry. Will you make us some cookies, please?"

Mimi laughed. "If you help me. I have an airplane cookie cutter—we could use that. But let's read a few more chapters, first, ok?"

"Finally!" Grant said. "Stop keeping us in suspense."

Christina picked up the book to read aloud and give Mimi a break. "Then stop talking," she ordered, and began to read.

13

EVENING, THE ELIZABETHAN GARDENS

The need had been building in him, so after school, Jeremy headed for the Elizabethan Gardens. His friends thought the gardens were sissy, old-lady, and tourist stuff. But he had loved to come here ever since he was little, and his mom would pack a picnic and take him to the library and then to the gardens. They'd sprawl beneath a hundred-year-old oak tree to read and snack and nap and daydream.

Mr. Midgett, the superintendent, would always come by and show him a new flower.

He'd talk about it just like it was a person and explain how it would grow and mature and what it would look like later and what he was doing to be sure it turned out just right. He cared for the flowers like they were his children.

Today was one of those rare warm spring afternoons that feel and smell so sweet that you could cry and laugh at the same time and not know why you were doing either.

Jeremy often felt yearnings and longings for something, but he wasn't certain for what. He only knew that his mind would seem to burst with ideas like new spring buds. When he was feeling this way, fuzzy bees and blinking butterflies seemed to make safer friends than people.

At the gatehouse, anchored to the corner of the garden with climbing roses, his problems did not seem to be allowed to follow him inside. He heaved a lavender sigh as he entered the garden created in honor of America's first colonists.

Maybe he could catch up on his speech. He knew a lot more about Indians than he did about writing, as Ms. Phillips never failed to point out. She would say he didn't have to do it her way, but in the tone adults use when they mean they'll be eternally disappointed, while thinking you're a lowlife deadbeat if you don't.

He didn't know how long he'd been writing, when he heard the snap of a twig behind him and spun around expecting to see Mr. Midgett. Instead, embedded in the sand beside him were two bare feet. Jeremy gasped.

Slowly and with dread, his eyes climbed the lean, brown, naked legs. At knee level, he swallowed hard, for the sliver-sharp point of an arrow quivered in the light of the setting sun.

Jeremy looked up past the loincloth, the painted red chest, and then, tottering precariously in the sand, his eyes met the fierce face of a wild Werowance—an Algonquian Indian chief from 400 years ago!

14
THE
WEROWANCE

Jeremy scuttled backwards like a frenzied hermit crab. As the stern Indian slowly lifted the bow and positioned the arrow, Jeremy rolled over into the thick brush.

As he squatted beneath the mountain of rhododendron, the sprung arrow pierced the flower above him and zinged on into the leafy forest. Jeremy stood and ran zigzagged through the garden.

Thudding footsteps gained on him easily, but he ran as fast as the thick and tangled, gnarled and knobby-kneed trees would allow. His heart pounded like war drums in his ears.

Now face-to-face with the statue of Virginia Dare, he'd made a wrong turn. How he wished the old legend would come true and she'd turn into a white doe and guide him safely out of the forest.

Swifter than sound, an arrow sped past him and clinked against the marble. Jeremy tore through the brambles and briars, ghostly hands of Spanish moss grabbing at him. When he reached the main gate, it had already been closed and locked for the night.

Without hesitation, he wedged painfully up the cyclone fence that separated the Gardens from Fort Raleigh and heaved himself over and into a thorny bush.

He willed his weary body to rise and fight the forest. The sound of straining fence and muffled grunts of its climber forced him on. Tears of exhaustion and fear trickled down his face.

Slowly, he crouched his way around the star-shaped, earthen works the colonists had built to protect themselves from the very enemy who tracked him now. Only the darkness had caught him so far and offered some protection from his pursuer.

Without warning, Jeremy tumbled blindly down the cascade of wooden bleachers of the waterside theatre. Each summer for more than forty years now, Paul Green's Pulitzer Prize-winning play about the colonists was performed here under the stars.

For a moment, he let his scratches savor the cool, soothing grass of the stage. Cautiously, he rose on all fours to crawl to his escape. Just a few more feet and he would vanish like an actor to safely, backstage.

Instead, Jeremy discovered the fear that a suddenly-blinded animal knows. Someone had thrown on the bright klieg lights and there, center stage in a spotlight of blood red light, he was exposed to his enemy.

100

15
THE
ELIZABETH II

Jeremy and Dennis scooted from one street corner to another in the dark. Only the slapping of the rising tide against the bulkhead kept them company.

The Lizzy II, as they preferred to call the ship, looked like a fat-bellied dragon just waiting for them to come close before exhaling fiery puffs through its cannon gills. It was its last night to sleep at Shallowbag Bay. Tomorrow it would sail.

Jeremy knew that if he didn't sneak on board tonight and search for his grandfather's coins, he would never have another chance. His interest had been renewed when that night in Fort Raleigh, the Indian had never reappeared, but the lights had beamed down not only on Jeremy but another 1937 coin.

The lowered gangplank should have been a warning, but the boys clambered aboard anyway. The creak of the timbers made Jeremy nervous and he wished the moon would come out and supplement his fading flashlight.

Below decks, the weak glimmer of light scalloped its way around the walls. It would take a while to check the trunks and casks. Methodically, they began to pry open the props of a 16th century voyage. Nothing.

"Hey, this trunk's deeper than the others," Dennis said.

"A false bottom?" Jeremy hoped, leaning over and prodding so hard with his flashlight it flickered out.

He squealed as a hard hand forced him face-first down into the dark hole and slammed the lid. Next he heard an instant replay as Dennis met the same fate nearby.

Jeremy hunched his shoulders and pushed upward 'til the flimsy trunk lid sprung open and he stood like a dazed jack-in-the-box. "Dennis?" he called.

"Over here," a voice quivered. But the answer had no meaning in the midst of a dark roomful of possibilities.

"Breathe slow!" Jeremy warned. If his grandfather's coins had been hidden when the hold was suspiciously sealed, the thief had probably just reclaimed them. He had to get them now or never. He groped his way up the ladder in the darkness and plodded along the deck. Something felt strange. A flash of heat lightning told him what—they had set sail!

16
THE
SHARKTOOTH
SEA

A thought so terrible came to Jeremy that he cried out. Were he and Dennis alone on this unleashed vessel? Or was someone pirating this ghost ship? He wasn't sure which he preferred!

The answer was instant. Like ghosts rising up in the night, the sails silently climbed the mast to slap at the sky. Echoing the grumbling thunder, he could hear two voices argue. "You were only supposed to . . ." one complained into the wind.

"We'll get it back to shore," the other bossed. "Don't worry."

Those voices! Jeremy knew them. They were from the fishing docks, boys just recently out of school. One was a troublemaker, the other a nice kid working his way through the local community college so he could go on to the university at Chapel Hill. They had always seemed unlikely companions, and his parents had always wondered what common interest associated them. The younger brother of one sat next to him in class.

What were they doing here, Jeremy wondered? Had they been captured too? An accident? Coincidence? It was hard for him to comprehend that anyone he knew might be involved in this mess.

Then the first teardrop of rain struck him on the neck and he squashed it like a fat, full mosquito. Pink lightning ripped ugly jags through the sky. Jeremy dashed for cover. One sail fluttered to the deck like a dead gull. A cry and a thud told him that one of the boys had been downed by the falling bed sheet.

At the wheel, the other boy groaned as he tried to hold hard to the swaying ship. On jellyfish legs, Jeremy hurried to help. If they ran aground on the treacherous sandy shoals that filled the shallow sound, they'd all be another statistic in the annals of ship-wreckery.

Misunderstanding his intentions, the boy lunged at Jeremy, who ducked as the body fell toward him. Then he heard the fading wail and punctured splash as the boy fell overboard into the Sharktooth Wave Sea.

COOKIES AND CRUMBS

Christina finally finished the next chapter, and she, Grant, and Mimi headed into the kitchen to start making cookies.

"I'll be in charge of the chocolate chips," said Grant.

"That means one for the cookie and one for your mouth, right?" his sister guessed.

"Right!" her brother agreed, already sampling from the large bag of chocolate chips Mimi always kept on hand.

As Mimi mixed the dough and Christina cut out airplane-shaped figures and placed them on the cookie sheet, Grant added the chips. Soon, Christina noticed that half the time he was missing the cookie completely. "Are you awake, Grant?" she asked.

"Yeah," Grant said. "I just can't quit thinking about the story. So, Mimi, is there really a real place called Rodanthe?"

"Yes, Grant, there is," Mimi answered, wrist-deep in cookie dough.

"And they really celebrated Christmas on the wrong day, and all those beast things really happened?" he pondered aloud.

Mimi handed the rest of the dough to Christina and washed her hands. "That's why they call it a legend, Grant. Perhaps it's true, perhaps not. What do you think?"

Grant said, "I think I like the idea of hanging my stockings twice! But I would not like to run into Old Buck...and get bucked, or something." He plunked down a few more chocolate chips, then, tossed a few in his mouth.

"Grant!" Christina scolded. "Well, I'd like to go to the Elizabethan Gardens. They sound so lovely and romantic," she said dreamily.

"You mean an ugly, ole boy might jump out and kiss you?" Grant teased.

"You're the only ugly, ole boy I know," Christina said.

As Mimi shoved the last pan of cookies into the oven, she turned and said. "Don't you two want to know what happened to the man who fell into the 'sharktooth wave sea'?"

"You bet!" squealed Grant. And as the cookies began to bake and smell ever so good, he volunteered to read the next chapter.

17
THE SOUND
AND THE
FURIES

Jeremy stood anchored to the deck, his mind racing like a runaway computer choosing and discarding an endless list of things to do, not do. Should he save his suffocating friend below first? Tend to the mutilated body swallowed by the fallen shroud? And, what about the poor soul overboard? Could he do anything before the ship slammed to smithereens upon the shoals?

The last vestiges of the surprise storm shook the ship in a rugged test of its premature seaworthiness. Thunder bellowed around him like the ghosts of pirate voices. Jeremy charged toward the wheel that twisted like a game at a circus midway. He had to save this ship, if only to show that it could have carried any colonists to any new worlds, new lives.

But his will was not enough. Sea spray blinded him. Like some medieval torture, the fly-by-night wheel wracked his spindly arms, as the sea cooperated in the duel between boy and all the powers nature can bring to bear when angered. Still he hung on, knowing splinters would only serve as slim shadows of the truth. But the pouting moon and the petulant sea joined forces to wrest the wheel from him and force him to the deck.

And then, two icy skeletal hands grasped Jeremy in the aching hollows beneath his arms and lifted him. The ship's wheel sandwiched between them, he found himself face to face with the drowned boy, much alive and as terrified as he.

But the wily wind would have nothing of this and snatched their slimy hands away. To their wonderment, a ghost rose up from the deck and floated towards them. Then the sail shroud slipped away to reveal one more bruised, battered and fearful boy.

Jeremy turned his futile watch at the wheel over to them. Taking a deep, wet breath, he slid down the waterfall to the lake in the hold below.

As fast as he could, Jeremy threw open trunks and thrust his numb arm hopefully inside each. Nothing. Empty. Then, a cold, small face filled his outstretched hand. An unmoving face, but at least he could feel the cool coming and going of breath in the center of his palm.

"I'm seasick and I wanna go home," Dennis cried.

Jeremy sobbed in relief and hugged his soggy friend.

18
ICE PLANT ISLAND

The sea was as smooth and pink as the inside of a conch shell; the sky a mirror of the sea. The water was as still and silent as a dreamless sleep, a lost thought. Only the subtle bulge of the single sail above and the clearing features of the figures on shore gave any hint of progress from the passage of the awful night to the unknown fate of morning.

On deck huddled four ragged, weary boys. On shore was a solemn row of inquiring eyes. They too were pink, but was it a reflection of the peaceful morning or the remnants of last night's lightning in those sockets? Jeremy feared he knew.

They all knew whose names would be called terrible today. Last night, after the storm had finally subsided enough for them to get control of the ship, the four boys had had a chance to talk.

In the cold, hungry hours between midnight and morning, it had come to light that the two boys on board were of Indian descent. They'd had the younger brother spy on Jeremy in class after his speech title was announced.

"*Those Whose Names Were Terrible* could only mean more put-down of native Americans," one had explained.

"We just assumed that you were going to make us all look like dumb heathens and savages," the other confessed. "We thought if we could scare you, you'd drop the whole thing."

"Didn't you ever think about just coming up and talking to me about it?" Jeremy had asked. "So I could explain."

"That never did the Indians any good," they told him, but agreed that they were wrong and ashamed and sorry after Jeremy told them the real nature of his speech.

He still didn't understand why they'd stolen his grandpa's coins and they did not seem to want to admit the real reason.

Before they could discuss it further, they'd all somehow found half a way to get comfortable, even if not dry, and fall asleep. By the time they awoke, the shore and their parents were in sight.

Those Whose Names Were Terrible, is all Jeremy could think. Savages. He suspected that's what the adults watching and waiting with folded arms thought about them all. And then the bow bumped the shore of Shallowbag Bay.

Safe . . . sound . . . and in very big trouble—they were home.

19

DAWN, MANTEO

Forever. Forever is how long Jeremy was sure they had been sitting in the Town Hall explaining and re-explaining what had happened. The why of the whole thing gave the adults a lot more trouble. But the persistence of the parents and the patience of the exhausted boys had finally made the matter halfway clear.

"Well, like most of the rest of the world's problems, this one seems like a lack of communication," summarized the sheriff.

"Where are my grandpa's coins?" Jeremy demanded.

As the boys plunged into soggy pockets and piled the silver coins noisily upon the desk, Dennis raised his head. "Go," he said, still half asleep, "Go buy us some breakfast, Jerm."

"We weren't going to keep them," the boys swore. "That's why we were on the ship. We'd hid them there a long time ago and knew we better get them off before today. Then if you'd given an anti-Indian speech we were gonna use them to pay to print our own version."

"And go on TV, too," the other blurted.

The adults tried unsuccessfully to hide their smiles.

"Well, I think the next chapter in this saga should include dry clothes and food," Jeremy's mother said.

"But what about the ship?" asked the flustered captain.

"We worked so hard to bring it back in one piece," Jeremy said, looking for forgiveness.

"We?" questioned the sheriff.

The boys looked at one another and grinned. "It took all of us," they admitted in unison.

"Except me," said Dennis. "But I was decapitated."

"You do mean **incapacitated**, I hope," Mother said. "How were you boys planning to spend summer vacation?" she added.

The boys exchanged glances of dismay. Dennis pretended to go back to sleep. "Earning money to pay for the damage?" Jeremy guessed.

"Close," said mother. Briefly, the boys had hope. "Now re-punctuate that sentence with a period instead of a question mark and you'll be exactly right."

Now there was no disagreement. Together, and loudly, yet relieved it was all over, the boys groaned.

20

THE 400TH!

Jeremy had given his speech. His two former enemies had been the first to congratulate him. "A little too long," one complained.

A few trillion tourists had come and gone and 400 years ago was now just 400 years and one ordinary day, but a pretty good day at that.

The Lizzy II had sailed (again!) and was safely berthed at Ice Plant Island. The silver coins, except for one which grandma had gone ahead and given him as a reward for a "speech well-done," were safe in a bank deposit box.

After the ceremonies, Ghost Boy and Drowned One, as Jeremy and Dennis liked to call them, returned to scrubbing the paint off the tombstones in the British Cemetery. He and Dennis had taken to going over and teasing them and even helping scrub a little too.

Today, in honor of the occasion, they brought a cooler of lemonade and some peanut butter and baloney sandwiches.

"Hey," Jeremy said as they wound their way down a path. "What would you want engraved on your tombstone?"

Dennis rolled his eyes at the gross thought. "How about FEED ME?"

Jeremy stopped in the middle of the road and swung the thermos thoughtfully. "I think I'd put GONE . . ."

"But not forgotten?" Dennis guessed.

"No," Jeremy said, slowly. "GONE . . . BUT NOT LOST."

"That sounds mysterious," Dennis said. "I don't understand."

Jeremy shrugged his shoulders. "I guess I don't either, but it sounds sorta like the truth. Race ya'," he cried and trotted off.

As he approached the graveyard, he thought he could see a few familiar faces. Queen Elizabeth grinned and nodded.

Blackbeard, head tucked in the crook of his elbow, waved jauntily.

What he didn't see was that he was being followed by others. The fleet-footed Manteo caught up and slung a weightless arm of wind around Jeremy's shoulder.

Ahead, Dennis plopped unknowingly into Virginia Dare's lap. "C'mon, slowpoke," he cried to his friend.

A little reluctantly, Jeremy picked up his pace and ran toward the future as hard and fast as his legs would carry him.

THE END

LOST AND FOUND

"Wow," said Christina. "That was a great story, Mimi. I never thought how much fun it might be to read a book with characters in it besides me and Grant. I feel like I met your Manteo friends in real life, and lived their adventure along with them."

Grant munched on his fifth chocolate chip cookie. Crumbs clung to his chin and a crescent moon shape of chocolate surrounded the dimple on his cheek. "Well, I'm jealous. I wanted to be in the story. I wanted to go to Manteo and Ocracoke and Rodanthe, and Kill Devil Hills. I wanted to sail on the Elizabeth II. It's not fair."

Mimi laughed. "Life's not always fair, Grant. That's just a fact of life."

"Yeah, it wasn't fair for the Lost Colonists, was it?" Christina said. "They disappeared. And I guess it wasn't fair for the Native Americans, because later, they pretty much disappeared, too, didn't they, Mimi?"

Mimi nodded. "Life was hard back then. It took a lot more explorers and colonists to finally get the New World settled. It wasn't always a pretty picture. There was plenty of starvation, bloodshed, disease, and bad weather. And, as if all that wasn't bad enough, the Golden Age of Piracy came along and folks on the coast had to cope with marauding buccaneers. It was always something!"

"Did you ever get to sail on the Elizabeth II?" asked Grant.

"No, not sail on it," Mimi said, "but we did get to go aboard when it was brand new. It smelled so good, like juniper trees after a rain. And they had kids just your ages aboard acting as sailors from that era. One kept following me around and talking to me."

Grant looked surprised. "Were they bad? Did they bother you?" He was always eager for another mystery to solve.

Mimi shook her head. "One boy did pester me a bit," she admitted. "He kept saying weird things to me in Elizabethan English."

"Like what?" Christina asked.

"Like 'Me thinks I never forget a face,'" Mimi said.

"Me thinks that makes no sense," said Grant.

"What was he trying to tell you?" asked Christina.

Mimi laughed. "That he knew me! I almost never figured it out."

"Why didn't he just say he knew you?" Grant asked, puzzled.

"Because he was supposed to stay in character," Mimi explained. "He could not say that because he only knew me in the future, not in the past."

"Huh?" said Grant, reaching for another cookie. Mimi slapped his hand.

"Who was the boy?" Christina asked.

Mimi smiled. "A boy who had been a character in an earlier mystery I'd written. Only he'd grown so much, I didn't recognize him!"

"Well, me thinks I'm still hungry for cookies," hinted Grant, walking his fingers toward the plate like a stalking spider.

"Well, me thinks it will be time for lunch soon," said Mimi, "so NO MORE COOKIES."

Suddenly the kitchen door burst opened and Papa bounded inside. "Lunch?" he said, grabbing a cookie—chocolate chip was his favorite. "How about oysters for lunch? Oysters as big as my forearm?" He held out his arm.

"No, thanks!" said Christina.

"NO, THANKS!" said Grant.

Mimi glanced up at Papa with a suspicious look in her eyes. "What's up?" she asked.

Papa grinned. "The Mystery Girl! Or she soon will be if we get over to the airport!"

"She's fixed?" squealed Christina.

"We can go on our trip?" Grant hollered.

"YAYYYYYYY!" they cried together.

"The parts came in and the repair was made, and we're good to go," said Papa, "so let's go!"

Instantly, there was a mad scramble to grab anything they needed and get the house ready to lock up.

"We can go see all the places in the book!" Grant told his sister, as they packed the car.

"We can swim in the ocean, climb Kill Devil Hills, and walk around Manteo, and see the Elizabeth II, and..." Christina listed. "And I'm sure Papa will fly us out to Ocracoke Island!"

"Oh, we don't want to do that," said Mimi. "We want to drive the skinny road by the ocean and take the ferry boats from island to island; that's more fun."

"What we want to do is hurry up," said Papa, closing the doors. "We have a good-weather window and plenty of light, so let's not waste them."

"And, the oysters are waiting?" Mimi added, with a twinkle in her eye.

"BIG AS A MAN'S FOREARM!" promised Papa with a big smile.

Together, Christina and Grant gave their reply to that, "ARRRRRGGGGGHHHH OOOOHHHH GRRROSSSS!"

HISTORY'S A MYSTERY

History's a
   mystery
   to me;
Sometimes
   in the
   past, there
   are things I
   can't see;
Why the colonists would
   disappear
Is not very clear,
Cause history's a
   mystery to
   me.

I often wonder how things came to be:
Why didn't those colonists carve more on
    that tree?
There is much debate over their fate;
Why so very clean did they have to wipe
    their slate?
That makes history a mystery to me.

How can a beginning have such a
    quick ending?
Were they so saddened to have to
    abandon . . .
With a blank final
    chapter, did they
    live happily ever
    after?
Oh, history's
    a mystery
    to me.

I keep trying to
    understand, but I
    keep losing my way;
Does anyone really know
    what happened
    yesterday?

Could what happened to them—happen to
me?
History's a mystery to me!

OVERTURNED TOMBSTONES

Overturned tombstones
Mark the place
Where restless ghosts
Begin to pace.

Who can blame them?—
Smothered in sand,
To wish again
To roam the land

Of beginnings
That they made,
Only now,
To haunt a
    grave.

AUTHOR'S COMMENTS

There's a lot of truth in this book. As you probably know, many of the places exist, and America's history really does date back four hundred years to when the first English colonists set foot in the New World on the North Carolina coast.

The Outer Banks is a very unique place where you can just feel the past all around you, even in the midst of modern-day activities such as surfing and hang gliding.

The two main characters were modeled after the sons of a friend of mine who lives at Manteo. I have personally been at the Island Inn on Ocracoke when the power went out! And, yes, I do think the Indians were treated unfairly, and still are today. I, myself, am part Cherokee, and you may have read of recent complaints by descendents of the ancient Indian tribes from this area, and from others.

While I'm usually an action-oriented writer, just the nature of this place made me spend more time on portraying the atmosphere and emotions felt in the story. So, you see, if professional writers can find ways to improve their writing, you can too!

I enjoyed writing this book and hope you enjoyed reading it.

I thought about you, the reader, while I was writing and tried to keep in mind the things you tell me you like in a mystery. I hope I succeeded!

Carole Marsh

Now...go to
www.carolemarshmysteries.com
and...

- Add this book to your personal Adventure Map Tracker!

- Go on a Scavenger Hunt!

- Take a Pop(corn) Quiz!

- Hear from Mimi, Papa, Christina, and Grant!

- Talk to Christina and Grant!

- Join the Fan Club...and MUCH MORE!

GLOSSARY

agitated: deeply troubled emotionally; upset

choreograph: compose a sequence of dance steps, usually to music

escapade: a carefree episode; adventure

founder: to fill with water and sink; to become wrecked

gnarled: knotty and misshapen; made rough by age or hard work

invigorating: giving strength, energy, and vitality

nautical: having to do with sailors, ships, or navigation

petulant: irritable; grouchy

premature: occurring before the proper time

remnant: a small portion that remains after the main portion no longer exists

shoal: a sandbank in a stretch of water that is visible at low tide

vestige: a trace or sign left by something that is no longer present

SAT GLOSSARY

atrocity: an act of shocking, terrible cruelty

feign: to pretend with the intention to deceive

heirloom: something that has been in a family for generations

incapacitated: deprived of strength or ability; disabled

verbatim: using exactly the same words

Enjoy this exciting excerpt from:

THE MYSTERY AT Mount Vernon

Home of America's First President, George Washington

1

CHOP PHOOEY

Christina felt tense for no good reason. It was springtime in Washington. The cherry trees throughout the city, a gift from Japan many years ago, were covered with blooms that reminded her of thousands of tiny, pink butterflies. The sun was shining, and birds were singing like rock stars. Still, something wasn't quite right.

Christina and her brother Grant had been to the nation's capital many times with their grandparents Mimi and Papa. Each time, her dream of visiting Mount Vernon, home of America's first president and Revolutionary War hero, George Washington, had never happened. But this time, Mimi had promised.

Papa pushed his cowboy hat back on his head, leaned against a cherry tree, and sighed. "When that woman finds a library, she loses all track of time," he grumbled.

Mimi, a mystery writer, had spent most of the week at the Library of Congress. She was researching a new mystery—one so mysterious she wouldn't even tell them what it was to be about. Christina had a sneaking suspicion it had something to do with the Revolutionary War.

Papa glanced impatiently at his watch. "Sure hope she didn't get lost," he said.

Grant had gone into a nearby toy shop to kill time while Christina and Papa waited for almost an hour outside a bike rental shop near Washington. It wasn't their usual way of getting around, but what better way to get to Mount Vernon and at the same time enjoy the area's most beautiful season?

Christina had just noticed black clouds on the distant horizon when a sudden whirlwind scooped cherry blossoms off the sidewalk and sent them in a pink blizzard straight toward her. Blinded, she froze as something grabbed at her shoulders.

Christina blinked hard but saw nothing but a fuzzy, gray blur passing her face. Was a rascally raccoon playing pranks on her? Another hard blink revealed a glint of silver from a hatchet blade. Raccoons don't carry hatchets, Christina thought in panic. Is there a madman on the loose?

"Papa!" Christina screamed, stumbling to the spot where she had last seen her grandfather.

Papa caught Christina just as she tripped. "Whoa there, little darlin'," he said in his deep, charming cowboy voice. "You know I love to dance with ya, but is the sidewalk the best place?"

"Someone's after me," Christina stammered and grabbed Papa around the waist. "And he's got a hatchet."

Christina felt Papa's belly jiggling with laughter.

"I think you better look again," he said between good-natured guffaws.

Christina rubbed her eyes. The fuzzy, gray image came into focus. It was only Grant!

"Looks like your brother has found some nifty souvenirs," Papa said with another laugh.

Grant struck a pose with the hatchet. What Christina had thought was a raccoon was a gray wig like old men wore in the 1700s.

"Guess who?" Grant said.

"A little old lady having a bad hair day?" Christina suggested.

Grant frowned. "If you knew anything about history, you'd know I'm George Washington," he said.

"You may think you're George," Christina replied, "but I cannot tell a lie. You've got that wig on backwards. The ponytail is supposed to be in the back, not coming out of your forehead."

Grant eyed the blossoms that had landed on Christina's shoulders. "Well, you should really do something about your bad case of pink dandruff," he said.

"Ha, ha, ha," Christina replied, rolling her eyes and brushing the blossoms from her shoulders.

"Here goes!" Grant shouted, raising the hatchet into position to give the nearest cherry tree a chop.

"Grant!" Mimi yelled. "Stop!" She scurried toward them, her red high heels wobbling on the cobblestone sidewalk. "Don't you dare hit that tree!"

Grant shot her a **mischievous** grin. "No worries, Mimi," he said. "It's only plastic."

"You need to do some more research on that cherry tree tale," Mimi said. "Most historians believe the famous story of a young George Washington chopping down his father's favorite cherry tree and then telling him the truth never really happened."

"You're kidding!" Grant said with a disappointed look.

"That's right," Mimi confirmed. "A preacher named Mason Weems used that story to teach boys like you not to lie."

"Guess that means I can never tell Christina how beautiful she is again," Grant said with another mischievous grin.

"If we don't mosey down that trail," Papa said, "those black clouds are going to rain on our parade."

Mimi changed from her red heels into her red tennis shoes. Of course, Papa had also rented a bike in her favorite color. As they buckled their helmets, the bike shop owner stepped outside to see them off. An old man with cloudy blue eyes, he gave them a warning that Christina thought was as **ominous** as the clouds.

"I'd be careful if I were you," he said. "There have been some strange things happening at that old mansion."

2
WAYWARD WIG

"Beat you to the top!" Grant hollered. He wheeled his lime green bike past Christina and pedaled hard. The gray ponytail of his wig wiggled furiously under his helmet.

"Don't forget, it's not called Mount Vernon for nothing!" Christina yelled after him. While waiting for Mimi, Christina had studied the trail map. She knew this final climb would be the worst, so she paced herself. She wasn't planning to let Grant win. She knew the best way to beat him would be to let his blast of speed wear him out long before he reached the top.

Christina waved to Mimi and Papa, lagging like Sunday drivers far behind, and stood up on the pedals of her blue bike. The springtime air was unusually humid and heavy for April, and it made Christina's shoulder-length, brown hair bushier than Grant's wig. At least I'm not likely to run into any of my friends, she thought.

Grant had almost reached the crest of the hill when he stopped and planted his feet on the pavement. Christina smiled with satisfaction. She knew her brother would run out of steam before he won the race.

"What's the matter?" Christina crowed as she flew past. "Run out of gas?"

Grant didn't reply. Christina pumped the pedals and gasped when she reached the crest. Standing stately beyond a sea of freshly mown grass was perhaps the United States' most historic home—Mount Vernon. The simple, white mansion with its red roof practically glowed in front of the dark clouds that still threatened their visit.

"Can you believe that George Washington actually slept here?" Christina asked her brother. He gave no answer. "Grant?"

Her brother had plenty of time to catch up by now. Christina looked in her bike mirror. She could see Grant's bike on the trail edge, but he was nowhere to be seen!

Christina knew Grant could never pass up an opportunity to use the bathroom outdoors. He had probably slipped behind a bush to do just that. But the bike shop owner's warning still swirled in her head. Christina turned around and aimed her bike back down the hill. "Grant!" she called. "Where are you?"

Naked branches just sprouting green buds clawed at Christina's clothes while she pushed through the brush beside the trail. "You better not be hiding!" Christina warned. She braced herself, waiting for Grant to jump out and say, "Boo!" Nothing happened.

"You can't scare me, I know you're here somewhere!" Christina yelled. She took more careful steps but stopped with a squeal. Something furry was tickling her toe.

"OOOOOH!" she yelped, expecting to see a wild animal about to bite her foot. What she saw frightened her even more. It was Grant's gray wig.